Butterfly Meadow

Zippy's Tall Tale

Come flutter by
Butterfly Meadow!

❋

and the next Butterfly Meadow
adventure . . .

Butterfly Meadow

Zippy's Tall Tale

by Olivia Moss
illustrated by Helen Turner

SCHOLASTIC INC.

New York Toronto London Auckland Sydney
Mexico City New Delhi Hong Kong Buenos Aires

To Remy Smet, the butterfly who hurt her wing but is flying again

With special thanks to Narinder Dhami

ISBN-13: 978-0-545-11242-0
ISBN-10: 0-545-11242-7

12 11 10 9 8 7 6 5 4 3 2 1   9 10 11 12 13 14/0

Printed in the U.S.A.

First printing, June 2009

Contents

Butterfly Meadow

Zippy's Tall Tale

CHAPTER ONE

A New Arrival

"Oh, I can't wait to hear what happened next!" Dazzle gasped. She settled down on a silky red poppy and looked at the glowworms sitting on the grass below her. "Go on, tell us the rest of the story."

Tonight, Dazzle was staying up late with her best friends, Skipper, Mallow, and Twinkle. The other butterflies in the meadow had already gone to sleep, but Dazzle and her friends were perched on wildflowers in the middle of Butterfly Meadow. The glowworms had come to join the fun, too! They were telling the four butterflies how they'd escaped from a lizard who was trying to eat them.

"He chased us all over the field," one of the glowworms said. "We were so scared! He kept snapping at us with his forked tongue."

"Did he catch you?" asked Skipper, her eyes wide.

"No. We spotted a really thick clump of grass," another glowworm explained. "We hid there so the lizard couldn't see our glow. Eventually, he went away."

"What a close call!" Dazzle said with a tiny shiver.

"Ooh, my turn!" Twinkle called excitedly. She fluttered around, her red-and-blue wings shining in the glowworms' light. "I've got a wonderful story — it's called *The Day My Wings Looked Especially Beautiful*."

Dazzle tried not to giggle. Twinkle was a peacock butterfly, and she was *very* proud of the colors on her wings.

"It was a sunny day," Twinkle began. "I was flying through a field not far from here, when I saw something *magical*."

"What?" Dazzle asked breathlessly.

Before Twinkle could go on, she was interrupted by a loud rustling noise. A patch of grass nearby began to sway — but there was no breeze! Just then, Dazzle spotted a glint of orange among the green. Suddenly, a big orange-and-black butterfly rose up from between the blades of grass. He flew to a flat rock nearby and settled there, batting his magnificent wings slowly up and down. He glanced at the other butterflies and the glowworms, his eyes twinkling.

"Hello!" Mallow called. "Welcome to Butterfly Meadow."

"Hello to you, too!" the butterfly called back. Dazzle could see that there were black bands speckled with white spots around the edges of his orange wings. "My name's Zippy, and I'm a monarch butterfly. I'm migrating south." He sighed heavily. "But it's such a long way! I've flown hundreds of miles, and I haven't spoken to any other butterflies for *ages*."

"I'm Dazzle, and these are my friends, Skipper, Mallow, Twinkle, and the glowworms," Dazzle explained. "Would you like to join us?"

Zippy cleared his throat, looking happy. "Well, I *was* listening to those stories you were telling," he said eagerly.

"I have the most exciting story to share with you. It's about the time I wrestled a bear."

Dazzle couldn't wait to hear Zippy's amazing story!

CHAPTER TWO

An Invitation

Zippy glanced around to make sure that everyone was listening.

"I was flying over the mountains during one of my long journeys," Zippy said. "Lots of scary creatures live there, and you have to keep your wits about you."

Dazzle was fascinated. She'd never been to the mountains!

"I was just minding my own business," Zippy went on, "when a wild bear appeared right in front of me. He growled loudly, like this — *GRRRR!*"

"What's a bear?" Dazzle whispered to Skipper, embarrassed.

"It's a great big shaggy animal," Skipper told her. "Bears have sharp teeth and a loud growl, and they love honey. They're very dangerous."

"I guess the bear thought I'd be a tasty snack," Zippy said, looking around at his audience. "He tried to grab me, but I dodged his enormous paw. Then we started to wrestle —"

"You *wrestled* with a bear?" Skipper cut in, surprised.

"I know you're a big butterfly, but a
bear is HUGE," Mallow pointed out.
"No butterfly could wrestle a bear
and win."

"Ah, but there's wrestling, and
then there's *butterfly* wrestling," Zippy
replied triumphantly, batting his wings
to and fro.

Dazzle, Mallow, Skipper, and Twinkle

looked at each other in confusion. The
glowworms began giggling and
whispering.

"What's butterfly wrestling?" asked
Dazzle, flying closer so she wouldn't miss
a moment of the story.

"Bears have extra-ticklish noses,"
Zippy explained. "I just brushed my
wings against that grumpy bear's nose
and tickled him.
He fell down
laughing and
couldn't get up
again." He
puffed his chest
out proudly.
"That's quite a story,
isn't it?"

"Yes, it is," Mallow murmured to

Dazzle. "I'm not sure I'd call that *wrestling*."

Dazzle could tell that her friends thought Zippy's story wasn't totally true, but she didn't care. She'd never met a butterfly like Zippy!

"Time for bed, I think," Skipper said with a yawn. "Nice to meet you, Zippy. Good night, everyone."

But Dazzle didn't want to go to bed. She still had so many questions to ask!

"You must have visited lots of different places," Dazzle said as her butterfly friends flew off to their favorite plants and the glowworms' light faded in the distance.

"Of course!" Zippy replied. "I've seen the highest mountains and the deepest rivers, and I've met hundreds of different

13

butterflies." Zippy yawned. "I need to get some sleep," he said, stretching out his wings. "I have to get an early start."

"OK," Dazzle said. "I'll show you a leaf you can sleep under. Where are you going tomorrow?"

Zippy followed Dazzle over to a large bush covered with purple flowers. "I'll

fly straight up and over the mountain beyond Butterfly Meadow."

"It sounds like a wonderful adventure." Dazzle sighed.

Zippy landed on a flower and looked closely at Dazzle. "Would you like to come part of the way with me tomorrow, Dazzle?" he suggested. "I can tell you lots more stories then, and show you some wonderful sights."

Dazzle's eyes widened in surprise. "I'd love to!" she said eagerly.

"Meet me at the edge of Butterfly Meadow first thing in the morning," Zippy told her, tucking himself under a leaf. "We'll go off on an adventure."

"I'll be there," Dazzle promised, bursting with excitement. Tomorrow, she was going to see the mountains! She did

15

a few happy twirls
in the air. Then she
danced over to join
her sleeping
friends.

"Dazzle?"
someone
whispered.

"Oh, Mallow,
are you still
awake?" Dazzle
looked up and saw
Mallow perched on
a leaf above her.

"Yes. I heard
you talking to
Zippy," Mallow
replied. "You
know, I'm not sure

it's a good idea to go looking for adventure *too* far from Butterfly Meadow."

"I'll be careful, Mallow," Dazzle said quickly. Suddenly, she had an idea. "Why don't you come with us, too?"

Mallow shook her head. "I'm happy here in Butterfly Meadow," she said with a smile. "Good night, Dazzle."

"Good night, Mallow."

Dazzle settled down beneath a comfy leaf. She was lucky to have a wonderful, caring friend like Mallow, but she still wanted to go with Zippy. Adventures were waiting for her — Dazzle was sure of it!

CHAPTER THREE

Heading Out

The next morning, Dazzle woke up as
dawn was breaking. The rising sun cast
a rosy glow over the meadow as Dazzle
flew through the mist to meet Zippy. She
was ready for an adventure!

Some of the animals who lived in the
meadow were already awake. There
were even rabbits nibbling at the grass as

Dazzle flew by. But the other butterflies were still asleep, and Dazzle cast an anxious glance over her shoulder as she left Mallow, Skipper, and Twinkle behind. She was excited, but she also felt a little guilty that she wouldn't be spending the day with her friends. At least Mallow knew where she was going.

I'll be back by midday, Dazzle thought as she headed toward the edge of the meadow. *They won't even miss me!*

But Dazzle couldn't help remembering the first day she'd left her cocoon. She'd been so lonely before she met Skipper and came to Butterfly Meadow. This would be the first time she'd be away from her friends since that first day.

Zippy was perched on a tree stump at the edge of the meadow, waiting for

Dazzle. He opened and closed his wings in the morning light, and Dazzle thought he looked awfully brave. She couldn't keep her own wings from trembling.

"Don't worry, Dazzle," Zippy said with a smile. "I'll look after you. Come on!"

Zippy zoomed up into the air, and Dazzle followed.

"It's a long way to the mountain," Zippy told her as they flew through a wide green valley. "But I have lots more stories to pass the time." He pointed a wing at some tall plants with huge pink

flowers and sword-shaped leaves. "See those gladioli plants? I've drunk nectar from flowers *twice* as big."

"Really?" Dazzle was very impressed.

"And I can fly *really* high in the sky," Zippy went on. "So high that I disappear. Watch me!"

Zippy darted up into the sky while Dazzle hovered below him. Fascinated, she watched as Zippy got smaller and

smaller until he dodged out of sight behind a cloud. A few seconds later, he flew out the other side of the cloud and fluttered down to Dazzle's side.

"I *told* you I
could fly really
high. I flew so
high that I
disappeared!"
Zippy said,
looking pleased
with himself.

"Er — yes," Dazzle said kindly.
*But Zippy only disappeared because he
flew behind a cloud,* she thought with a
little smile.

The pair flew on, over rivers, through
valleys, and across fields. Zippy pointed
out different plants and animals to
Dazzle, and told her more wonderful
stories. But after a while, Dazzle's wings
began to feel tired.

"Are we far from the mountain, Zippy?" she panted.

The monarch butterfly laughed. "Not at all," he replied. "Just look up!"

Dazzle raised her head. Her heart began to thump with excitement — they'd reached the foot of the mountain!

Gray and rocky and steep, it stretched
high above them. The peak was covered
in glistening white snow.

Dazzle was amazed by how big and
cold the mountain looked. She suddenly
felt very, very small.

CHAPTER FOUR

A Surprise Encounter

"Don't worry, Dazzle," Zippy said. "I know you're used to the warmth and sunshine of Butterfly Meadow, but it's not so bad up there."

"Are you sure?" Dazzle asked.

"Of course," Zippy replied. "Come on!" He began to fly along the steep side of the mountain.

Dazzle followed, looking around curiously. The air smelled sweet and fresh, and the grass below them was very green.

"Look at the flowers!" Dazzle peered at the pink and purple plants that clung to the rocks and tumbled down the mountainside. "They're beautiful."

"See the waterfall over there?" Zippy called over his shoulder.

Up ahead, Dazzle could see a waterfall rushing down the steep, rocky face of the mountain. The blue water sparkled with silver in the sunlight.

"Oh!" Dazzle cried. "I've never seen anything so wonderful."

"And see the tall tree near the water's edge?" Zippy pointed out. "That's a beehive, full of delicious honey!"

Dazzle saw that the tree had a hole in the trunk. There were bees buzzing busily in and out. It reminded her of an adventure she and her friends once had with a lost honeybee named Sting. Dazzle felt a little pang of sadness — she missed her friends in the meadow!

As the two butterflies flew higher, the air became colder. Suddenly, Dazzle realized that she was slowing down. Her wings were so cold!

"Zippy, you said it wouldn't be too bad up

here," Dazzle said with a shiver. "But it's freezing! I can hardly move my wings at all."

"Just keep moving," Zippy said bravely. "That'll help you stay warm."

Dazzle glanced at her new friend. She could see that *he* was flying more slowly, too.

"I think we should leave the mountain now," she said anxiously. "We're both tired. Plus, I must leave before it gets dark. Otherwise, how will I find my way back to Butterfly Meadow?"

Just then, the ground began to shake. Dazzle heard a loud, grumbling growl echo across the mountain. Frightened, she glanced around. What was making this scary noise?

She soon had her answer. A huge animal with shaggy brown fur lumbered out from behind a tall rock. Dazzle gave a gasp of fear.

"Now we're in trouble," Zippy said weakly.

"What kind of animal is it, Zippy?" Dazzle asked, fluttering beside him. Then she remembered what Skipper had told her the night before. "Is it a . . . *bear*?"

Zippy nodded, looking frozen. As the butterflies watched, the bear reared up and stood on his hind legs. Now he looked even bigger! Dazzle and Zippy shrunk back behind a raspberry bush, trying to hide among the leaves. The bear was staring right at the bush. His

black eyes lit up as he spotted the two little butterflies.

"Zippy!" Dazzle cried as the bear headed straight for them. "You have to protect us!"

CHAPTER FIVE

Being Brave

Zippy stared at the bear. His face turned pale.

"This is awful!" he groaned, wriggling farther and farther inside the raspberry bush.

He's trying to hide! Dazzle realized in dismay. But hadn't he already defeated a bear once before?

"Zippy, help me!" Dazzle cried. Her heart sank. The bear was getting closer and closer. She could see his long claws glinting in the sunlight. By now, Zippy had flown even deeper into the bush, his wings trembling. *It's all up to me*, Dazzle thought. *Zippy's too frightened to do anything but hide. I have to protect him!*

Dazzle thought of what Zippy had said about tickling the bear's nose with his wings. "I'll give it a try," she murmured, shaking all over. "Zippy!" she called. "Let's go bear wrestling."

But Zippy just shook his head and ducked out of sight.

With a deep breath, Dazzle flew out of the raspberry bush and headed straight

38

toward the bear. He growled loudly, his eyes sparkling with anger. The bear had huge, furry paws with sharp claws, and long white teeth. Quickly, Dazzle headed for his nose.

"Get away!" the bear roared, swiping at Dazzle with his paw. She darted safely out of reach.

"Oh, please listen!" Dazzle cried breathlessly. "Butterflies are *very* small. We'll never fill your huge stomach!"

"*Grr*, I don't want butterflies for breakfast," the bear growled grumpily. "I want to get even with that silly orange butterfly." He pointed at the raspberry bush where Zippy was hiding.

"Zippy?" Dazzle asked, surprised.

"Yes, he was teasing me with his wings last time he was here." The bear glared angrily at Dazzle, fluttering in front of him. "And now you're doing the same thing."

"Oh, no!" Dazzle whispered. "I've made things even worse."

With that, the bear made a grab for her. Dazzle had to dodge sideways to escape his paws.

"Zippy, you have to be brave and help me!" Dazzle cried as the bear lumbered after her.

But there was no sign of her new friend. Dazzle was on her own.

CHAPTER SIX

Bees to the Rescue!

The big bear swiped at Dazzle again. As she dodged aside, an idea popped into her head.

"Skipper told me that bears love honey," Dazzle murmured. "Maybe the bees will help me if I lead the bear to their hive?"

It was her only chance. Perhaps the

bear would be distracted by the delicious honeycombs and leave her alone!

Dazzle flew swiftly down the mountain, toward the waterfall.

"Come back here!" the bear called after her. "I'll show you what happens to naughty butterflies who tickle my nose."

Dazzle didn't slow down. She could hear the bear crashing through the undergrowth, grumbling and growling

behind her. Dazzle risked a quick glance over her shoulder. He was following! But Dazzle could feel the air getting warmer as she went farther down the mountain, so she could fly faster.

The bees were still busy collecting pollen and buzzing in and out of their hive when Dazzle reached the waterfall.

"I'm so sorry to disturb you," Dazzle panted, zooming over to the bees' tree,

"but I'm being chased by a grizzly bear!" She jumped as the sound of the stomping, tromping bear came closer.

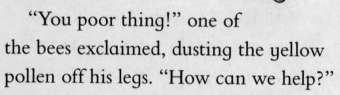

"You poor thing!" one of the bees exclaimed, dusting the yellow pollen off his legs. "How can we help?"

"Well, bears like honey," Dazzle explained, as a group of bees buzzed around her in a friendly way. "I know that you build these hives to hide your honey from grumpy old bears. But do you think you could spare a bit, to help me distract him?"

"Sure," one of the bees agreed. He zipped over to the hole in the tree and

shouted, "Hey, come out! There's a
butterfly here who needs our help."

Dazzle backed away to a safe distance
as more bees swarmed out of the nest.
There were so many that Dazzle thought
they looked like a big black cloud. Their
loud buzzing filled the air.

Suddenly, the ground shook as the
bear thundered through the trees
toward them.

"He'll take our honey," Dazzle's new bee friend whispered. "But he's done that before. We can make more. And at least we can help you out — and have fun with him first." He turned to the other bees. "Come on, guys!"

Quickly, Dazzle settled on the branch of a nearby tree, out of the way. A moment later, the bear appeared beside the waterfall. He growled loudly, looking angrier than ever.

"Where's that butterfly?" he snarled.

Immediately, the bees surrounded the bear and danced around his head, buzzing loudly. Dazzle was amazed. The bees didn't seem scared at all! The bear shook his huge furry head to keep them away.

"Even bears don't like bee stings!" one

of the bees shouted to Dazzle.

A moment later, the cloud of bees swirled up into the air and flew away.

"It's about time!" the bear grumbled. "Now, where's that annoying butterfly?" He glanced toward the beehive, and Dazzle saw his face light up.

"Honey!" he roared.

From her hiding place, Dazzle could

see a trickle of honey running down the trunk of the tree. The bear rushed over and dipped his paw inside the hive. Then he pulled out a dripping handful of glistening yellow honey. He licked it greedily off his paw.

The bear forgot all about me, Dazzle thought, relieved. She flew off after the bees, leaving the bear with his honey. "I wonder what happened to Zippy?"

CHAPTER SEVEN

A Guilty Conscience

"Wait!" Dazzle called, hurrying to catch up with the bees. "Thank you so much for helping me."

"You're welcome," the bees buzzed together. She watched as they flew off, waving cheerfully.

A flash of black and orange caught

her eye. Dazzle could hardly believe it. Zippy was flying toward her!

"Hello there," Zippy called calmly, floating down to rest on a rock. "Where did you go?"

Dazzle blinked. "I was trying to lead the bear away," she said. "Why were *you* hiding in the raspberry bush?"

"I wasn't hiding," Zippy replied, looking hurt. "Didn't you see that big

green snake slithering near the bottom of the bush? I had to wrestle him, or he would have swallowed us both whole."

Dazzle gazed doubtfully at Zippy. Why was he making things up again? But Dazzle was too tired to argue.

"I'd better head home now," she said. "It's a long way back to Butterfly Meadow."

"I think I'll come with you," Zippy replied. Was he looking . . . guilty? "Maybe it wasn't such a good idea to fly over the mountain. I think I'll go *around* it instead. But first, I'll make sure you get safely back to Butterfly Meadow."

"Thank you, Zippy," Dazzle said.

"And thank you," Zippy said quietly. "It was really brave of you to lead that bear away from me."

Dazzle shook her head and smiled. Even though he'd left her to deal with the bear on her own, Zippy wasn't so bad.

Together, the two butterflies flew down the mountainside.

Dazzle spread her wings, enjoying the warm sunshine as they got closer and closer to the ground. Then she spotted three familiar shapes bobbing in the air below them.

"Oh!" she cried joyfully. "It's Mallow, Skipper, and Twinkle!"

CHAPTER EIGHT

Reunited

"Hello!" Dazzle called.

"We came to look for you," Skipper called back.

Dazzle bounced happily through the air toward her three friends. They danced around each other, smiling.

"I'm sorry I left without saying good-bye this morning," Dazzle said.

"Well, we weren't angry, since Mallow knew where you'd gone," Twinkle replied. "But we thought you might like some company for the long trip home."

"Did you enjoy your adventure?" asked Mallow.

Dazzle glanced over her shoulder at Zippy, who'd stopped for a drink of nectar.

"Well, I've learned one thing," Dazzle whispered. "Zippy's a fantastic storyteller, but I'm not sure how much of his stories is real, and how much of them is made up."

Her friends looked at each other and laughed.

"We know what you mean," Mallow said.

Just then, Zippy zoomed over to them.

"Hello," he called. "I bet I can
guess what you're all talking about.
Dazzle's telling you how I wrestled a
snake that was going to eat us, right?"

"Did you see this wrestling match,
Dazzle?" Skipper asked, grinning.

Dazzle shook her head. She decided
not to mention that she'd been escaping

from a grizzly
bear at the time.
She could tell her
friends about
that later!

"Oh, it was
terrible," Zippy
said dramatically.
"The snake
wrapped itself around me and tried to
squeeze all the air out!"

Dazzle smiled as Zippy went on
talking. Even though Zippy told a lot of
tall tales, Dazzle knew that he didn't
mean any harm.

"Well, now that your friends are here
to take you home, Dazzle, I'll be on my
way," Zippy said as they reached the
foot of the mountain. "Thank you for

coming with me today." He gave a little
sigh. "I get lonely sometimes when I'm
on a long journey."

Dazzle nodded. She realized now that
Zippy spent a lot of time on his own. He
just got a little carried away with his
stories when he met other butterflies.

"I've had some wonderful adventures

today, Zippy," she said gratefully.
"Thank you for inviting me."

"Good-bye!" Zippy called, his
orange-and-black wings fluttering as he
headed around the side of the mountain.

"Good-bye!" Dazzle and her friends
called after him. When Zippy was out of
sight, Dazzle turned to Twinkle, Skipper,
and Mallow. "I have a story to tell you
on the way back to Butterfly Meadow,"
she said.

"What is it?" Skipper asked eagerly.

"Well, it all started when Zippy and I
were resting in a raspberry bush," Dazzle
began.

Dazzle told her friends all about the
bear and the bees as they headed back to
Butterfly Meadow. The journey seemed
to go by in a flash. Dazzle could see why

Zippy liked telling stories so much —
they really helped to pass the time!

"That sounds awfully scary." Twinkle
sighed as they flitted over the swaying
grasses of Butterfly Meadow. "But now
you're home safe and sound, Dazzle."

Dazzle nodded. She'd had lots of
exciting adventures with Zippy, but she
was glad to be back with her friends.

"Home is where the heart is, after
all," Skipper said.

"And my heart is right here in
Butterfly Meadow!" Dazzle agreed.

❃ FUN FACTS! ❃
Butterfly Vacation

Imagine going on vacation to somewhere you've never been before — without a map! You must travel thousands of miles no matter what the weather. You have no coat or hat and no place to stay. Now imagine you're a butterfly.

Seems impossible, doesn't it?

But millions of butterflies make this difficult journey each year. They leave their homes in late August and early September and fly thousands of miles to get away from the cold weather. This journey is known as migration.

Monarch butterflies fly from Canada to as far south as Mexico. They fly well over 2,000 miles for sunnier weather.

Other butterflies, including the red admiral and the painted lady, also migrate, but none as far as the monarch.

The butterflies' trip can be dangerous. They must battle the wind and rain as well as dangerous creatures. They can travel up to fifty miles a day.

No one is exactly sure how these butterflies know when or where to migrate because butterflies only make this journey once in their lifetime. Pretty amazing for these tiny little creatures!

Dazzle is at home in

Butterfly
Meadow!

Here's a sneak peek at her next
adventure,

Skipper Gets Spooked

CHAPTER ONE

Strange Butterflies

Dazzle laughed as she raced around the
big oak tree after Mallow and Skipper.

"Wheeee!" Twinkle cried, whirling
through the air nearby.

"What's next, Mallow?" Dazzle asked.
The four butterflies were flying home
after a day at Cowslip Pond, and Mallow
had suggested a game of follow the leader.

She was the leader, of course — she loved telling her friends what to do!

"Try this!" Mallow flew in a zigzag pattern, fluttering her small white wings.

"Can I be the leader next, Mallow?" Dazzle panted. "I thought of some great things we could do." Dazzle loved the idea of leading the others through the woods!

"Sure, soon," Mallow promised. She hopped from daisy to daisy, yellow pollen dusting her feet. Her butterfly friends bounced after her.

"Oooh!" Mallow skidded to a stop, fanning out her wings. The others piled up behind her.

"Whoops!" Skipper giggled. "I almost crashed into you, Mallow!"

Mallow didn't answer. Instead, she darted behind a nearby tree, and her three friends followed. They crowded next to Mallow, who was peeking around the tree trunk.

Mallow pointed one wing toward something in the distance.

Dazzle, Skipper, and Twinkle all stuck out their wings, laughing. They were following the leader!

"*Shhhh*," Mallow whispered. The other butterflies *shhhed* her right back.

"No, look over there," Mallow interrupted. "I mean it — look!"

At last, the three butterflies realized that Mallow wasn't playing anymore. They peered around the tree. What was Mallow pointing at?

RAINBOW magic™

There's Magic in Every Series!

The Rainbow Fairies

The Weather Fairies

The Jewel Fairies

The Pet Fairies

The Fun Day Fairies

The Petal Fairies

The Dance Fairies

Read them all!

■ SCHOLASTIC

www.scholastic.com

www.rainbowmagiconline.com

RMFAIRY